Words to Know Before You Read

Let's Learn The **Ss Blends** Sound

sled	snail
slide	snow
slope	snowboarding
slow	standing
small	stay
smell	sticks
smoke	stop
snacks	

www.rourkeeducationalmedia.com

Edited by Precious McKenzie
Illustrated by Ed Myer
Art Direction, Cover and Page Layout by Tara Raymo

Library of Congress PCN Data

Sledding in Summer? / J. Jean Robertson
ISBN 978-1-62169-275-1 (hard cover) (alk. paper)
ISBN 978-1-62169-233-1 (soft cover)
Library of Congress Control Number: 2012952781

Rourke Educational Media
Printed in the United States of America,
North Mankato, Minnesota

Educational Media

rourkeeducationalmedia.com

customerservice@rourkeeducationalmedia.com • PO Box 643328 Vero Beach, Florida 32964

SLEDDING in SUMMER?

Counselor
Soni

Counselor
Brad

Andee

Cole

Grace

Sid

Willa

Yari

Written By J. Jean Robertson
Illustrated By Ed Myer

"Yippee," yells Yari. "We're going sledding!"

"How?" asks Cole. "It's summer. There's no snow."

Counselor Soni says, "When it's summer in the north part of the world, it's winter in the south part."

4

CAMP ADVENTURE

SLEDDING SLOPE

Counselor Brad says, "No one should be standing. Please stay in your seats. Snap your seat belts snugly. Our helicopter-bus is ready to lift off."

CAMP ADVENTUR

"Do we get to try snowboarding, too?" asks Grace.

Counselor Brad smiles, "We'll just have to wait and see."

"This chopper is slow. It is creeping like a small snail," sighs Cole.

Counselor Soni says, "Try sleeping while we fly. It's a long way to Peru."

When they get there Sid shouts, "Snow! I love snow!"

"We are slipping and sliding down the slope with sleds," says Andee.

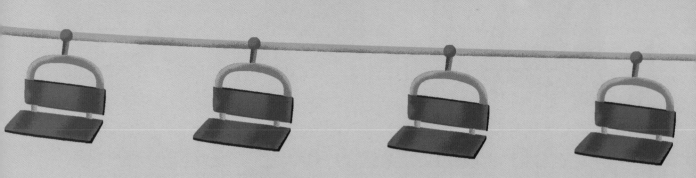

"Let's ski!" says Sid.

Away they go! Down the snowy slope!

"Snowboarding is the best. I don't ever want to stop!" says Grace.

"Sledding is my favorite," says Yari.

"I smell smoke!" cries Willa.

"Look!" shouts Cole. "It's a bonfire and we're making s'mores for our snack."

"Yum! S'mores are good!" shouts Sid.

After Reading Word Study

Picture Glossary

Directions: Look at each picture and read the definition. Write a list of all of the words you know that start with the same sound as *smoke, snow, stop,* or *sled*. Remember to look in the book for more words.

 **sled** (SLED): A sled is a vehicle you can ride on in the snow.

 **slope** (SLOPE): A slope is the downward slant of a hill.

 **smoke** (SMOKE): Smoke is the cloud of burning matter from a fire.

 **snacks** (SNAKSS): Snacks are little treats of food between meals.

 **snow** (SNOH): Snow is the form water takes when it falls from the sky when it is very cold outside.

 **snowboarding** (SNOH-bord-ing): Snowboarding is a sport where you use a flat board to stand on and slide down a hill.

About the Author

J. Jean Robertson, also known as Bushka to her grandchildren and many other kids, lives in San Antonio, Florida with her husband. She is retired after many years of teaching. She enjoys her family, traveling, reading, and writing books for children. She loved to go sledding on the hill by her home when she was a child.

Ask The Author!
www.rem4students.com

About the Illustrator

Ed Myer is a Manchester-born illustrator now living in London. After growing up in an artistic household, Ed studied ceramics at university but always continued drawing pictures. As well as illustration, Ed likes traveling, playing computer games, and walking little Ted (his Jack Russell).